The Other Way

Other books by Caperton Tissot

By The Way, 2020

Pirates on the Saranac, 2019
(A children's story)

On Thin Ice: The Life of a North Woods Caretaker, 2018

Kicking Leaves: The Contrarian Life of a Yankee Rebel,
2018

The Beat Within: Poetry Another Round, 2017

Adirondack Flashes and Floater: A River of Verse, 2014

Saranac Lake's Ice Palace: A History of Winter Carnival's
Crown Jewel, 2012

Adirondack Ice: A Cultural and Natural History, 2010

History Between the Lines: Women's Lives and Saranac
Lake Customs, 2007

Books available at your local bookstore and on Amazon.

More information and contact at
www.SnowyOwlPress.com

The Other Way

A Short Story Collection

by

Caperton Tissot

ISBN: 978-1-916696-38-9

PublishNation LLC
www.publishnation.net

One way is fast, efficient, predictable.
Just for joy, try the other way...

Acknowledgments

I am deeply indebted to my husband for his excellent editing, as well as to Diana Krautter for her meticulous proofreading. I am also grateful to my reading group for their detailed feedback. Without all of you, this book would not have been possible.

Table of Contents

Mr. Stuart Jones

Eyes glued to the road, he reached down and switched on the radio. After a spill of raucous music, he was treated to the following announcement: "Mr. Stuart Jones, president of the Quimsby Bank, passed away today. He was just 45, in the prime of his life…" He bent forward, intent on not missing a word and, momentarily distracted, barreled right though a red light. Fortunately, he hit no one. Horrified at his carelessness, he pulled over to the roadside, turned off the motor and took a couple of deep breaths to calm himself down. Suddenly it hit him what an absurd thing had just happened and he burst into laughter. After all, who gets to listen to his own obituary? How did that happen anyway? After sitting a minute longer, he had second thoughts. It had not been a very flattering description of his life. In addition to that, he had not, in fact, died. The situation began to anger him.

Pounding the leather encased steering wheel of his 1965 BMW, he shouted: "This is crazy! How dare you? What is the meaning of this?" But the newscaster had moved on to other things as if no mistake was possible.

"That's it? Just that? Come on. What about my accomplishments, what about all that, huh? All before age 45? Not bad! That's one lousy tribute!"

Stuart Jones started the car again and slowly drove home. Arriving at the usual time, he left his car on the circular drive at the front door, walked up the marble steps and into his house. The butler was waiting at the door, apparently unaware that Stuart was dead for he showed no surprise at seeing him at all. "Your drink is ready for you, sir," was all he said. Stuart marched into his burgundy walled retreat. Interior designers had created the perfect room: a large mahogany desk by the window, file drawers close at hand, ceiling-high bookcases holding leather bound sets of unread books all arranged by color, with here and there, strategically placed silver golf awards displayed to break up the monotony. "Golf awards for Christ's sake! Don't they count? And what about the Charleton-Parker merger I engineered as president of the board? Cut jobs, saved money – made millions for the shareholders! What about that?" he said to nobody because nobody was there. After picking up his Scotch and water and taking a large slug, Stuart picked up the phone book, looked up WPXY, grabbed the telephone and dialed.

"Good evening. WPXY. How can I help you?"

"Stuart Jones here. Give me the news desk!"

"I'm sorry sir. It's closed for the day. You'll have to call back in the morning. It opens at 6 a.m."

"That's not good enough. Give me someone now!"

"Sorry, sir, but there's no one to take your call."

"There must be a reporter somewhere!"

"They're out on their beats or home for the night. Please call back tomorrow." Click.

Stuart slammed down the receiver. "I'll be damned." Used to things going his way, he found the present situation intolerable. Leaning back in his desk chair, he grabbed his drink and took another long swallow before moving over to the easy chair where he could more comfortably fume at the world. *This means I'll be dead until tomorrow!*

The next morning, he was up at six, dialing the radio station. A secretary took the call. Stuart demanded to speak with the supervisor who came on the line. "Stuart Jones here," he bellowed, "There's been a terrible mix-up. I heard my obituary on the radio last night while I was alive and well, driving home from the office!"

"Excuse me, sir, your obituary?"

"You heard me! I want that retracted right now!"

"Yes, sir. I'll look into it immediately, sir. I do apologize. Of course, we'll need a written statement from you affirming you are alive and well."

"What?" exploded Stuart, "You're talking to me, aren't you. How could I be dead?"

"You have my sympathy, Mr. Jones, but we have to follow the rules. Now, I can send a runner over to your office with the form. You just need to fill it out, sign and send it back. That way we can take care of the matter immediately. What time will you be getting there?" Stuart Jones was steaming but saw no way around the absurdity. He was still in his silk robe, his watch on the bedside table. He picked it up and stared at it, as if it would tell him how long he needed to get dressed and breakfasted.

"Alright. I'll be in by eight. Send him over!"

At the station WPXY, the supervisor, Mr. Crumble, hung up the phone, left his office and marched into the newsroom where reporters and newscasters alike sat lined up behind typewriters. It didn't take long to figure out what had happened. The station kept a file of ready-to-go obituaries of prominent men and women so that when one of them gave up the ghost, WPXY would be the first to break the story. Apparently, in moving the file from one location to another, Mr. Stuart Jones's obituary had fallen onto the floor. The newscaster, getting ready for the 6 o'clock evening news, had picked it up, assuming it was to be part of his spiel. That newscaster caught Hell for his mistake. Mr. Crumble returned to his office, shut the door, sat down in his chair and, no longer able to contain himself, burst out in laughter. "The miserable stuffed shirt," he said to no one in particular, "Stuart Jones got what he deserved." He laughed so long the tears ran down his cheeks. His very own nephew was one of the men who lost his job due to the merger engineered by Jones.

At 8 a.m., Stuart entered the Quimsby Bank and strode toward his office. Two women stood giggling in the hallway but stopped when they saw him approach. "Good morning, Sir," they greeted as he passed by.

He reached his secretary's desk and asked, "I suppose you heard?"

"Yes sir, such a shocking thing," she replied with the hint of a snicker, her face hardly reflecting any sorrow at all.

The employees' reactions were not lost on him. It was even worse when he had to undergo the humiliation of filling out an official form denying his death, then signing and returning it by messenger.

That done, he announced to his secretary, "I'm leaving early today, reschedule my afternoon appointments. I'll be back in tomorrow."

His car was brought around to him from somewhere in the depths of an underground garage. He got in and drove off – but to where? *Got to get away alone for a while but what should I do?* Besides business and golf, there was little else in his life. *Maybe I'll try the beach,* he decided, *should be quiet this time of year.* He headed out of town for the shore.

It was a cold autumn Tuesday, the beach mostly deserted, the surf pounding, driven by a storm far out at sea. Stuart got out of his car and started walking. He noticed his shiny black shoes were gathering sand in all their precise little creases. He took them off, along with his socks, carried them in one hand and continued on barefoot, walking the beach for the first time since he was a boy. The air was fresh and salty, the cold lapping waves tingled his toes. He envied the gulls soaring overhead, seemingly free of worry. Why hadn't he thought to do this before? He took a deep breath, looked around and seeing nobody, flung his arms out to the side and started to run, laughing all the while. Not in great shape, he didn't last long and was quickly out of breath. Yet, he felt better than he had in years. Spotting a weather-beaten log above the tide line, he veered off in that direction, ready to sit down and catch his breath and rest.

He watched the waves break and tumble toward the shore but, inevitably, his thoughts reverted back to the radio announcement from the evening before: *fine upstanding citizen, engaged in civic activities, member of the Lawrence Country Club, president of the Quimsby Bank in Marionville, no survivors, parents and brother predeceased. God, was that it? My whole life in one boring paragraph. What kind of success was that? No mention of anything I've done for others.* He tried to think of things he had done for others. He couldn't. In fact, what did come to mind was the time his cousin developed multiple sclerosis, had to quit teaching and asked him for help. He had never answered her letter. *Guess I should have just as I should have found a* wife *and had a child to carry on my fine name. Is it too late now?*

Suddenly, Stuart heard screaming from out on the beach. Standing up to better scan the area, he saw a pregnant woman, dress blowing in the wind, wading into the pounding waves. He jumped up and ran toward her, nearly tripping over a red plastic bucket and shovel lying on the sand. "Damn it," he exclaimed.

"Help, my son's out there," she called, pointing into the waves.

"I see him," he shouted. A tiny head was visible about 100 feet from shore. "I'll go. Keep pointing in his direction. It may be hard for me to see him once I'm out there."

Oh my God! The last thing I want to do is plunge into that maelstrom. Then he did exactly that, tearing off his jacket before rushing into the frigid water. Paralyzing cold hit hard, momentarily taking his breath away. Recovering, he dove through the breaking surf as the green water churned and thundered in his ears. Coming out on the other side, he willed himself to stay calm, treading water and holding his head high to look around. Towering waves made it difficult to see far. It was disorienting. Where was the child? Then, he spotted the woman standing on the beach frantically pointing to the right. He was going the wrong way. Changing course, he swam in the opposite direction. It seemed an eternity before he spotted the flailing child bobbing up and down, black hair washing over his face. Stuart grabbed him just as the boy suddenly appeared to go lifeless. With his right arm around the kid's neck, holding his head up, he kicked his way toward shore, his left arm doing all the work. He had to swim back through the breaking surf, not letting go of the child, even though his left arm was starting to hurt badly. *Muscles complaining but I've got to hold this kid tight,* he told himself. Finally reaching shallow water, he was too weak to stand.

By this time, help had arrived. An ambulance was parked up on the road, the crew down at the beach. Somebody waded in and grabbed the child. Then he felt arms lifting him toward shore. There he dropped, out of breath but relieved to be sitting on solid ground. A blanket was thrown over his shoulders, someone checked his pulse.

Not ten feet away, he saw a white jacketed medic bending over the boy, a boy who couldn't have been older than eight. His mother stood watching, a man at each arm holding her up as she looked on, her beautiful face drawn tight with fear. The medic turned the boy to his side and began slapping him on his back. Suddenly, all the ocean taken on board came spewing out. The kid took a deep breath, coughed and coughed some more. His mother watched, tears of joy streaming down her cheeks. And that was all Stuart saw before another medic kneeled down beside him, blocking his view. But it was all he needed to see. "Ah, success," he murmured to himself.

"Taking you to the hospital. Like to get you checked out in the ER," said the second medic who now had a cuff wrapped around his arm and was pumping it, releasing it, tightening it again, watching with concern as he checked his pressure.

"Hey, I'm fine, don't need that," mumbled Stuart. Two stretchers stood nearby. The boy was strapped on one, Stuart, too weary to resist, loaded on the other.

The boy survived, Stuart did not, succumbing to what turned out to have been a heart attack.

………………..

It was 5 minutes before 6, Tuesday evening in the news room at WPXY. The newscaster, jumped up from his chair. "What the Hell is this obituary doing back on my desk?" he shouted. "I'll get fired for reading it again. It's all a mistake."

"Read it," the shift manager snapped back.

"Excuse me, but I don't think you understand. We've had a major screw-up here. This notice fell out of the file. I read it last night – nearly got fired for doing so. Don't want to do that again." With a minute to go, no time for further talk, the newscaster shoved it aside.

However, this time it was no mistake. The next morning, the Marionville Gazette scooped the station with a front-page headline. "Stuart Jones gives his life to save a Child." The article described his heroism in detail. It was all high praise. The last line was a quote from the mother: "I shall be eternally grateful to Mr. Jones for saving my precious son's life. In gratitude, I will name my next child after him. He has restored my faith in humanity which I had lost when my husband was laid off last year due to the Charleton-Parker merger."

A Shaft of Light

Alex left yet another girl at her doorstep. She barely muttered goodbye before hurrying inside. Was it his scarred face, his limp or his personality? Would he ever find a companion to share the coming years? Thirty-five already and he was still searching.

Alex was an occupational therapist. It was his job to bring people hope, show them how to overcome their disabilities, find a way to function in their daily lives. And yet, he himself found that difficult. A car accident when he was eighteen had given him a bad scar running from his hairline, down the right side of his face, leaving him with a droopy eyelid and a jagged red slash line across his cheek. It pulled one side of his mouth down into a grimace. He had been told that he'd never walk again. The prediction was wrong. Determined, he had struggled through physical therapy and learned to use his legs again, though his gait was somewhat lopsided, one leg being shorter than the other.

To amuse himself on the long, lonesome weekends, Alex browsed antique shops as well as the pawn shop on 22nd Street. Always on the lookout for deals, he often found them: an old book or an appealing piece of glassware. He rarely paid much for anything. That was the game – find hidden gems for cheap. His apartment on 44th Street was an eclectic yet oddly pleasing assortment of discoveries: a wooden cuckoo clock, a plaster bust of Mozart and several small bronze sculptures. One Saturday afternoon in March, while browsing through the pawn shop, his eye was drawn to a shadowy painting of the interior of a barn, a shaft of sunlight shining on a chestnut stallion. It was painted in bold strokes and yet suggested a lot of detail.

"Who's the artist?" he asked.

"Some starving amateur, no doubt. It's not signed. You can have it for a song – 25 bucks." It didn't seem like a song to Alex but he found the picture appealing, in fact so appealing that he bought it, spending more than he normally would.

………………..

The following Monday at the rehab center, he was assigned a new patient: Maggie Davis. Maggie had been left legally blind after a case of shingles had damaged her cornea.

"Good morning, Maggie," he greeted his new patient, an attractive slender brunette with a narrow face, slanted eyes and a turned-up nose. She followed him to his office, stepping tentatively along, not trusting her white cane. After getting Maggie seated, he took down her medical history, then asked, "What are your goals right now?"

"I'd love to get back to work; I need to make a living. But it's hard being blind. I have no idea what kind of work I could ever do again?"

"What did you do before this happened?"

"I was a fifth-grade teacher."

"It must have been hard to give that up. However, there are other job opportunities out there. We need to first find out what you can manage right now."

"Not much," she sighed, looking his way with her damaged eyes, "Everything seems impossible. My neighbor helps with banking, paying rent and grocery shopping but she's busy with a job and relatives. I can't be depending on her. I mostly just stay in my apartment and listen to the radio. It's no life."

"Well, I'm here to show you that there's a better future for you. You just need help getting there. So, let's get started." The hour went by quickly. Alex set up a plan to carry them through the next six weeks.

"After that, my insurance runs out," she told him, "I was able to keep it going for four months from the time I stopped teaching but, I can't afford to hold on to it any longer."

The next weeks sailed by, both for Maggie and for Alex who found himself increasingly taken with his patient. She had not had an easy life: an only child, parents dead, doing well as a teacher until she lost her vision. She was living off disability checks but those weren't quite enough to cover rent, food and bus fare to the therapy center.

"Tell you what," Alex proposed one day, "Why don't we schedule your appointments for first thing in the morning. This way, I can pick you up on my way to work. It will save you bus fare in one direction at least."

"That would be wonderful. Are you sure you won't mind?"

"Sure. See you Thursday at 7:40. I'll be waiting in front of your building."

Divorced at 23 after a short bad marriage, Maggie had spent little time around men since then. Now at 29, she was nervous about the prospect of riding with Alex. *Remember,* she reminded herself, *he's just giving me a ride because he feels sorry for me, nothing else. Besides, it's only a short 20 minutes to the center.*

Alex was just as nervous. *She surely is a sweet woman with a tough road ahead. This is the least I can do for her,* he thought, trying to pretend that that was his real motive.

Their first trip together was comically awkward and mostly spent chatting about the weather and how warm it was growing with the approach of spring.

Her progress in therapy continued slowly but steadily.

"You're getting there," he told her. "Keep studying braille, it's not just for reading but will expand your ability to get around. Everything from elevator buttons to signage to ATM machines is in braille. I'll also help set up your computer with braille keys and an audio app." Indeed, the world was opening up for her again.

The rides to the center rapidly led to a growing friendship. Maggie began to relax and talk more freely. She told Alex about an expensive corneal replacement operation which *might* fix her vision but her insurance wouldn't even begin to cover the cost.

"If only I could wave a magic wand and find the money, I would pay for that surgery in a heartbeat," said Alex.

"You are so kind. I know you would but as that's not going to happen, I need to get on with learning how to live well despite being blind."

Alex discovered a charming, cheerful soul, suppressed until then under the grief of losing her vision. With his encouragement, she made progress with therapy but six weeks passed far too quickly.

"Why don't I continue to work with you at my place? That way it will be free."

"You'd do that? I mean, that would be very time consuming. I don't want to interfere with your after-work hours."

"I don't think of it as interference." And so, Alex maneuvered them into a more intimate setting – and relationship. When he laid his hand on hers to guide her to a task, it lingered a little longer than needed. Under his tutelage, she became increasingly independent, blindness holding her back less and less every day. She was immensely grateful to him. For Alex, this was the woman he had dreamed of: caring and kind. Therapy took on new dimensions when it moved into the bedroom.

....

One day, Maggie received a letter which she brought to Alex to read. A distant cousin had written that a great aunt of Maggie's had died several months earlier. The family, in going through her papers, had learned of the existence of a valuable painting done by a famous artist. However, no one could remember what had happened to it or what it depicted. Did Maggie, by any chance, know anything about it?

"Oh my God! I did have a painting inherited from my mother's side of the family," she told Alex. "It was a favorite of mine but I didn't think it had any great value and it wasn't much use to me anymore. To help me get by, I recently sold a lot of stuff, including that painting. I hope it isn't the one my cousin is talking about."

"Where did you sell it?"

"My neighbor took it to the pawn shop on 22nd Street for me – didn't get much for it."

Alex opened his mouth in astonishment. Maggie, of course, was unaware of his reaction. Trying to avoid sounding too excited, he casually asked, "What was it a picture of?"

"A stallion in a shaft of light in a barn."

"Oh," said Alex, "Well, it probably isn't the one your uncle is talking about." *So, she loved this picture just as I do – another sign we are meant for each other. Should I tell her I bought it or first have the picture appraised?* He said nothing. The next day, unbeknownst to Maggie, he brought the picture to an art appraiser. It was as he had guessed, the missing painting. "I'll offer you $60,000 right now."

Alex, seriously conflicted, replied, "I think I'll wait. Got to think about it. I may be back later." *If he's offering that much right off the top, it must be worth a great deal more, enough to finance her surgery.* Home he went, returning the picture to its place on his living room wall until he decided whether or not to tell Maggie about it. *This find is a miracle, almost like it's meant to be. Maggie could have the operation and get her sight restored. How amazing. On the other hand... when she sees what an ugly lover I am, it will surely end our relationship and... my hopes for our future. Do I give all that up so she can see again? Of course, the operation might not work and then we'd just be wasting the money.*

What to do, tell her about the painting or not? Alex wrestled with his conscience for several days, became impatient with Maggie, as often happens when the victim is blamed for the crisis. But she was forgiving.

One day, they had completed her therapy session – the professional kind – at his apartment, when she turned to him.

"I think helping me after putting in long days at work is getting to be too much for you. Maybe we should stop with these sessions. After all, I can carry on from here. You've taught me so much. Look, I can now walk around your apartment without knocking things over," she said, standing and moving toward the hall where her coat was hanging.

"No!" he exclaimed, "It's not that."

"What is it then?" responded the gentle Maggie, turning back to reach out and lay a hand on his arm, "You seem overly preoccupied these days."

"I'm sorry, sometimes I get this way, will you forgive me? I want you to feel as comfortable here as I do." He gathered her in his arms and held tight as if a storm might pull them apart.

"Of course, darling. You spend so much time helping me, you're entitled to feel cranky." She finally released herself from his grip and stepping away, said, "I'd feel a lot more at home here if I knew more about the antiques you have collected to furnish your place." What kind of things turn you on?"

"Well, first of all, *you*. Beyond that, sure, let's take a tour." They started at an end table next to the sofa, Alex handing her first a miniature sculpture, then a basket, a candlestick. They moved around the room, Maggie picking up different objects and feeling them while he talked. Then she walked over to the wall and slowly ran her hands along it until she came to a frame.

"Now tell me about your pictures." He grew increasingly nervous as her hands slid along, touching each frame and asking for descriptions. He told her about a small print of a cottage on a heath, a watercolor of men harvesting hay and a pen and ink of a fisherman in a canoe.

"Let's stop now," he then said. There's nothing much else."

"Oh, but I have a lovely textured frame here," she said, her fingers running over intricately carved wood. "It reminds me of the frame on the picture I sold. Tell me about it."

Alex gave a deep sigh, ran his hands thru his short blond hair and paused a minute before speaking. "This one?" he asked, stalling for time as he stared out the window. "This is, a... a landscape with... with mountains and a river and..." then he stopped.

With a heavy heart he began again. "Actually, it's a picture of a stallion standing in a shaft of light in a barn...."

Alternative Facts

"Mr. Wilson called to say Irene wants me to get rid of the pink flamingos in my yard. Now, why would she ask that? Here I go and try to make the place all pretty for my neighbors."

"Ah, strange, that woman. I'd love to meet her someday but her husband says she's bedridden. You ever seen her?"

"Never, but her husband tells her everything. She sure doesn't miss a beat when it comes to knowing what's going on in this park."

"It must keep him plenty busy taking care of her, what with her stuck in bed and all. How old do you think she is? I mean, he's no spring chicken."

"Not sure having never seen her but I saw a box addressed to her in the postal room the other day. It was from Regina's Cosmetics so she cares what she looks like."

"Yeah, and I've seen several boxes there for her from the Slinky Dress Shop in Atlanta. Strange, why would you dress up if you're in bed all the time?"

"Mr. Wilson told me that she does all the book work. Couldn't be too sick if she does that."

"Well, she must be good with money. They don't seem to want for anything. Wonder what's the matter with her."

"Don't know but I do hear their dog barking up there on the hill. Who takes care of the dog if she's in bed all day and he's out working at the phone company?"

"Hard to say. I wish we could meet her some time. Must be lonely stuck in bed all the time with no one around for company."

"Yeah, but maybe she's not very friendly. Remember Irene sent a message to Julia that she was not allowed to get another dog after her pooch died? That was mean what with Julia so old and lonely."

"Hah, because of that, when Joy lost her dog, she got another one right away, looked just like the dead one. Fooled them she did. That Joy, she's real smart."

"By the way, how long you lived in this park?"

"Oh, been two years already."

"And you've never met Irene?"

"Nope."

"Me neither and I've been here longer. Strange. Think if she was so sick and bedridden, she might not be living no more."

"My friend Julia has a friend Tricia who knows someone named Linda who knows George, the postmaster. He told Linda who told Tricia who told Julia that Irene gets a disability check every month."

"Is that so? And Mr. Wilson says because his wife's so sick, he's had to hire a secretary to help out."

"So that's who that is. I saw a good-looking young woman driving around with him checking out our trailers the other day. Bet that was her."

"Was she slinky?"

"Now just what are you thinking?"

"Well, there *were* those boxes from the fashion store."

"Yeah. You may have a point – hired her for her looks, I'll bet."

"Can't trust those young 'uns to play square. I bet she's up to no good."

"Making a play for him, you reckon?"

"I do indeed."

"Think he'll fall for it?"

"Think he already has."

. . . .

"Guess what happened today? Mr. Wilson said he was going to be digging up some boulders out in the woods to use in his yard as a backdrop, said not to be getting all upset if we heard the excavator up there at night. Now who ever heard of putting boulders in your yard? Most folks want to get rid of them," announced Gertrude.

"No understanding what people like – boulders okay but not flamingos? Go on with ya."

"And why dig at night? Seems fishy to me."

"Maybe, though it's because it's the only time he can, being as how he works all day at the phone company."

"Somehow I doubt that's the reason. Very suspicious, the whole thing."

"I hear ya. But, it's tough to run a park and work full time. However, they must be doing very well, living in that nice house up on the hill. You ever see it?"

"Only once. They don't seem to like us going up there."

"Hey, I got a friend who wants to rent a trailer here. I told her she'd have to consult with Irene the Mobile Home Queen. But when she called the secretary answered and said Irene was too sick to talk. Do you believe that? I tell, you, there's something going on."

"When you think about it, Mr. Wilson's looking in better shape every day. Getting jollier too. Gertrude asked if he planned to expand the Park into those back woods. He actually laughed and said no, he liked it just the way it is."

"Ah, I noticed he bought himself a new car too. Seems to me he's acting like a young colt. There's only one reason a man does that."

"And him with a wife stuck in bed like that. Makes you mad to think about it."

"Yeah. It's a strange set up here. I mean the Park is looked after pretty well but that house on the hill might as well be in a different state for all we know. You got to wonder what they're hiding. Think they might be a bit friendlier. That new secretary, she sure doesn't say much. Bit of a cold fish, if you ask me."

....

Two days later, Joy, Julia and Gertrude stood chatting in the driveway by Julia's double wide. She had one of the nicer places, painted blue and white with flowers in a window box on the end facing the road. It was an orderly park with neat tiny lawns at the front of each lot, and only here and there a rust-streaked trailer marring the view – but what could you do if you were retired and short on cash? The Wilsons didn't seem to see it that way but then, "they were rich, what did they know?" A few trailers were rented but the majority were owned by the residents who paid monthly land rent.

"So, the way I see it," said Jack, an older resident who had joined the group. He paused to push his cap up, a sure sign a guy has something important to say. "Fishy stuff's going on there on the hill. I mean, we've never seen this supposed Irene, the Mobile Home Queen, and now suddenly there's a beautiful woman up there helping Mr. Wilson?"

"No kidding," chimed in Billy, another resident who looked about 40 and was wearing greasy coveralls, "Mr. Wilson brought his car to my garage the other day. Wanted it undercoated. Guess what I found inside? A gun in the glove compartment!"

"Oh Lordy!" exclaimed Julia, throwing her arms up in the air, "A gun? What's the world a-comin' to."

"And," said Joy, "it makes you wonder about all that digging at night."

"Not natural, something tells me."

"Honest people don't dig at night. More likely a grave he's getting ready."

"And all those disability checks? Wonder who cashes those in for his own gain."

"For sure there's something bad going on."

"Think we should call the police?"

"Not yet. We can't be certain though it sure don't look right."

"Yeah, let's wait a couple of days and watch. Everybody keep a watch out. This maybe big."

"I say there's evil walking these grounds. We best attack it soon."

"And I say we wait," like Billy says, "before we make a move. Let's catch him in the act."

After a little more chatter, the group broke up and went their separate ways with enough excitement to entertain them for several days. It made their scalps tingle just to think about it.

It wasn't long before the other mechanics at Billy's garage heard all the details of the latest "facts" making the rounds in the Park. Julia also relayed the gossip to Tricia who told Linda who told George, the postmaster.

Later that afternoon, while Joy was out walking her immortal pooch, she spotted smoke rising from the hill – a lot of smoke. A couple of other residents were standing smoking cigarettes.

"Look over there!" Julia shouted, pointing up the hill towards the woods shielding the Wilson's house. Isn't that smoke?"

"It surely is," answered one of the smokers, rubbing his hands together, "It's a fire alright. Call the fire department! Irene must be trapped inside. I'll take the car up there and rescue her!"

He was too late. The house was fully engulfed in flames. The fire engines arrived 10 minutes later. "Someone in there?" yelled the chief.

"I think so. There was a woman, bedridden."

"Ah, terrible! That place is already burnt nearly to the ground. We can't get inside anymore. Who's the owner?" Just then a police officer arrived and took down the information needed to contact Mr. Wilson. Meanwhile, the usual crowd of gawkers had arrived to make their opinions known on everything from the fire department to the "failing" marriage of the Wilsons. The fire pretty well clinched it. "Won't surprise me if they find a charred corpse once this cools down. Told you so."

That was Jack. Of course, he hadn't told anyone any such thing but why not lay claim to smarts when you have a chance? And, folks weren't apt to remember what he'd said anyway.

The next day, investigators arrived to determine how the fire had started. No charred corpse was found. Billy was there on his lunch break, standing around at the scene. One of the investigators strolled over to speak to him. "You know much about the Wilsons?"

"No sir, not really. But there's been some strange stuff going on around here."

"Like what kind of strange?"

"Well, I'm not one to talk about other folks, no, not me." He looked down at the ground and gave a sigh. "No, it's not like I want to tell on anyone but Mr. Wilson has been digging around in the back woods late at night. Sort of weird."

"Want to show me where?"

"I can't tell you exactly where, but my neighbor knows. He told me. I'll get him." The neighbor did not know but asked the woman who told him about the digging and she said she didn't know either but she knew the woman whose lot was closest to the woods. That woman led the somewhat skeptical investigators to the spot. There, sure enough, the ground had been disturbed. A thin layer of leaves had been raked over the dirt.

"Hah! They'll be digging up a corpse soon, mark my words" was heard around the park. It's murder for sure. The residents gathered nearby, like vultures watching for road kill. An excavator had been brought in and the digging begun. However, what they found was not a body but rather a large metal crate which, to the watchers' great disappointment, was not opened but loaded onto a nearby truck and driven away.

And where was Mr. Wilson all this time?

"Probably fled to another country," was the general opinion. "Always knew he was a bad un." However, Wilson had not fled but simply gone to the nursing home where his beloved wife Irene was being cared for. Guillain-Barre disease had her in its grip. Lately, she had taken a turn for the worse and needed extra special nursing care. The cost was extraordinary so the Wilson's daughter, who had been living in California, returned back East to help her father run the park. So much for the "sexy secretary". She had bought a house nearby where her father was now staying.

And what was in the large metal crate? It all came out in the paper two days later. The box was full of antiques: clocks, candlesticks, porcelain, mirrors and a few pieces of jewelry. The investigators immediately suspected arson on the basis that these valuables had first been removed prior to the fire. However, there was no concrete evidence of arson.

The insurance company refused to pay on the policy. Wilson took them to court. After days of deliberation, the jury came back with its verdict. Seems they were moved by the tragic tale of a man who had a desperately ill wife and whose bank account had been drained trying to care for her. The insurance company was ordered to pay up.

Did Wilson rebuild his home? No. He moved in with his daughter, bringing along his beautiful collection of antiques. The insurance money went towards providing his wife the very best care.

. . . .

Six weeks later, back at the Park, the neighbors had gathered together, this time on a Sunday in front of Billy's place. "Did you hear about Mabel in # 82? She was seen in town with a very handsome man, apparently a secret lover – husband seems completely unaware."

"Anyone know who the man could be?" Nobody did.

"You don't say?" said Jack. You never know what a person is up to behind closed doors. He's always so good to her – think we should tell him?"

"Maybe. We'd feel terrible if the boyfriend breaks down the door and murders the husband in cold blood and us never having warned him!"

Passing in the Night

Sometimes an inconsequential act leads to a consequential change. So, it was when I spoke up in the Red Tavern dining room early on a Tuesday evening on a Tuesday in May, 2010.

"I see you're eating alone," I called across the still empty tables and chairs. Would you like to join me?"

The heavyset woman looked my way, said nothing, then got up from her seat and lumbered over to my table. Gray hair and a lined face hinted that she had more years behind her than I did.

"Waitress, could you bring over her silverware and drink? Thank you," I said before turning to my new dinnermate who was settling in across the glossy wooded table in the small pine-paneled dining area. What possessed me to be so bold as to invite a stranger to dine with me? I had been wondering if I dared to do it, then realized I'd never know what I missed if I didn't.

"So, I'm visiting here to give a talk at the library," I said, "about tolerance and diversity in our culture. What brings you here?"

"Highbrow stuff," she said before continuing, "I'm an antique dealer, or you might say, a junk dealer looking for antiques. A lot of old homes around these parts. Folks are supposed to come to the community center tomorrow – bring their stuff for me to look at. I'll make an offer if any of it's worth anything. If it isn't, I'll at least try to tell them a little about their pieces. That way they'll go away with something, even if it isn't money."

"How interesting. Have you been doing this for long?" I asked.

"Yes, but mostly it was my husband's business. I just helped when I could. Taking care of three children, one of them disabled, kept me busy. Didn't leave me much free time."

"It *was* your husband's business, you said. What happened?"

"He died a couple of years ago. Left the business to me but not much else."

"Left you memories maybe?"

"Yup, but not too many good ones. Glad I'm free again, if I do say so and I *don't* say so to most people. They won't understand. Don't know why I'm telling you all this. I'm trying to turn the store from a junk shop into an antique store. Never had much schooling so I don't know how to do it real good. But it's tough getting by with little money and missing the kids. Never thought life would be so hard."

"I guess none of us did," I replied, aware that what I considered a hard life was nothing compared to hers.

"Pop was a railroad man. Didn't make much but we always had a place to live. Now just keeping a roof over my head seems impossible." A that moment the waitress arrived with fly speckled menus. My seatmate had been drinking a beer. She now ordered another. "I'll take a cheese-burgher and lots of fries," she added.

"Quiche for me, a side salad and a Malbec."

"One of those I see," she said, "Always eating healthy, staying slim. I can't be bothered. Food's my one fun these days – not about to give it up."

Despite lecturing on prejudice, I realized how, at heart, I was still pretty critical of people's choices. Wasn't that a kind of prejudice as well? It was past time I stopped. She clearly had had a tough life. Who was I to judge her eating habits?

"By the way," I continued, "My name is Daylia, what's yours?"

"Betty. I never heard of a name like Daylia before. Where'd you get that?"

"Family name. My husband's a teacher," I explained, "in a private school. Pay's not great. I have two sons: one's in college, the other dropped out and works as a welder. Not exactly the direction we thought he would go but he's okay with it. The boy who is a welder still lives at home. Seems to us it's time he move out. Young people don't seem to understand. At a certain age, paying the mortgage and putting food on the table is their own responsibility. The other boy comes home for vacations. It keeps us busy trying to finance it all."

I picked up my fork and cut off a tiny sliver of quiche. The slower I ate, the longer it would last. I watched my weight all the time, sometimes resenting the strict diet. My frequent presentations on television meant I was expected to stay trim and attractive according to the rigid and prejudice standards of media. It was a good job, pay not great but interesting. However, it required I travel a lot and that I did not enjoy.

"Sounds like a good life to me." she said.

Before I could answer, the waitress returned carrying a tray loaded down with our order. She set down another beer, and the cheeseburger platter. I caught her look of disdain at my overweight dining partner and felt defensive. Who was this slim young chick to sit in judgment of someone years older who she knew nothing about? Then she set my salad down on my side of the table, gave me a smile and, ignoring the older woman, asked if I needed anything else? Yes, I felt like saying, I'd like you to come to my lecture tomorrow – the topic has suddenly expanded to include types of prejudice I have previously overlooked. However, I said nothing, unwrapped my fork and knife which had been rolled into a flimsy paper napkin.

I took a sip of wine while my companion was busy grabbing for the ketchup bottle and liberally dousing her fries with the bloody mess. Spearing an impossibly long fry, she tried to stuff it in her mouth without much success. Then she looked up at me, jowls sagging,

"Where are *your* children now?" I asked her.

"Sadly, not at home anymore. One is retarded, or they tell me I should call it an intellectual disability. Whatever it's called, it's tough on her. I love Maria dearly but though her age is 20, she's sort of like a four-year-old, can't be left alone. I couldn't cope anymore after my husband died and I took over the business. I had to put her in a halfway house. Breaks my heart. I visit when I can. My older son Walt was a good student until he got into drugs and died at sixteen. The middle child, Michael, has done well for himself but moved away for his work. I don't blame him. He's a lineman living in Kentucky, married with two children but I don't see them often. He tells me he doesn't have much time to travel all the way north to the Adirondacks."

What could I say? How devastating. She had no family waiting at home and here I was complaining about my kids not leaving the nest. "Wow. You must be a strong woman to deal with so much."

"Oh, thank you, Miss. Nobody ever told me that before. I try not to complain but I get so weary. My son says I should move out of the house. It's falling down around me. But it's home and where would I go?"

"Where do you live?"

"Rabbit's Crossing," she told me, speaking unnecessarily loud for my overly refined upbringing. She continued in a loud raspy voice, "Not much there – nearest grocery store's 10 miles away. Most people moved out way back some time ago, even the rabbits are gone. Haven't seen one for a long time. Antique shop is on the highway outside town. Lots of tourists drive by looking at the scenery. Some stop and browse, buy a thing or two, just enough to help me keep going. Gives me some company too."

Betty picked up her cheeseburger, studied it for a minute, then took a big bite. It gave me a chance to study her more closely. Dark red lipstick carelessly applied gave her mouth the appearance of a wound; mascara was so thick her eye lashes stuck together. When she blinked, tiny black marks appeared below her eyes. Her cheeks were bursting with cosmetic color. Wiry gray hair fell to her shoulders. But the eyes – her eyes were large and brown, gentle and kind.

We continued to talk, trying to bridge the differences in our backgrounds, get on the same wavelength. I told her about my work and how important it was to me to encourage tolerance of diversity. I confessed to being discouraged at times, that I felt my efforts made little difference in the world – all things I had never admitted to anyone before. She reached out and laid a gentle hand on my arm.

"Don't feel that way," she murmured in a quieter voice, "Everything we do makes a difference. We may never know how and where but that's not a reason to stop trying. You have to believe this. It's the only way to keep going. We don't always know where goodness will land. Like, the other day, a staff member at the halfway house where my daughter lives told me Maria is very kind to the other residents. I taught her to be that way. Never knew if she had heard me. Guess she did."

"How heartening to hear those words," I said, "I mean, the staff's words and yours as well. I guess we don't always realize what effect we have on others."

"Well, I think you're a very nice lady," replied Betty. "I'll say that. I mean, you invited me to eat with you tonight. Nobody's ever done that before." We turned back to our plates. I slowed down a bit so we would both be eating at the same time. It took her a while to plow through all the "blood" spattered fries.

"Now for dessert," she finally announced. Dessert? I was full up. Thought she would be too but apparently not. I signaled the waitress, asked what they had. It was the usual: a choice of heavy cakes and pies and ice cream sundaes. Then she mentioned bread pudding.

"Bread pudding?" Betty exclaimed. "That's my very favorite. Bring me a bread pudding."

I couldn't image what the attraction of bread pudding was but to be friendly, I ordered one too.

When it was brought to the table, Betty looked at it a moment, then teared up causing her mascara to smear down her cheeks in a dreadful mess.

"What is it," I asked in alarm, wondering if she was finally breaking down.

"It's okay," she said, "It just always reminds me of Walt. This was his favorite dessert. Poor boy. Couldn't get him to stop with the drugs. Sometimes the grief just jumps up and bites me."

It was my turn to reach out and lay a hand on her arm. "Not your fault you know. Drugs are everywhere and it's easy to get addicted when you're young. It's a tough medical problem. Even the professionals have a hard top getting people off them. You did your best."

"Oh, but you don't know. I used to scream at him so hard he left the house for days. I just wanted him to stop. That's all. Instead, I pushed him further into the drug world..."

"You did not," I interrupted, "He drove himself into that world. Our own son had alcohol problems. It used to make me crazy too. I also did my share of shouting and fighting with him. But we were lucky we could afford counseling. It took a long time to turn him around even with the pros helping. How were you to do that by yourself?"

"I wanted to get help but my husband just said I was a nag – leave our son alone. He would figure it out. He was wrong. I should of never listened to him."

"Time to forgive yourself. You did all you could," I said, giving her arm a gentle squeeze, "Just remember all the good things about him." With that, I withdrew my hand and dug into the abysmal pudding. Lifting my spoon, I proclaimed, "Here's to Walt." She joined me and we finished those deserts in no time. After that we ordered coffee and, neither of us quite ready to leave, we chatted. Her background was so different from mine: little education, constant poverty, poor health, and yet, to my surprise, we shared much. Finally, getting late, we paid our respective bills and left.

"Goodbye, it was such a pleasure to have a meal together."

"Yes," she said. "That was real nice. Good luck with your talk tomorrow."

"And good luck buying antiques. Hope you find lots of them."

....

The next day, thanks to meeting Betty, my talk deepened to include a much-expanded exploration of tolerance and risk taking. An image came to mind of the ocean, stormy at times with waves pounding vessels and wind tearing at the rigging, other times, lying calm and tranquil. We live as if sailing an unknown sea. Conditions can change without warning. But, for one quiet moment, Betty and I found solace. Like two lonely ships passing in the night, we hailed each other before moving on with more steam and our lights a little brighter.

Stigma Static

"She's all good, my wife, couldn't find better," declared Jonathan as the three families gathered in the back yard for a 4th of July barbecue.

Sarah sighed inwardly. *If he ever knew who I really am, I don't think he'd be boasting like that.* Despite her unease, she managed to smile.

"Of course, he didn't look far. Worcester isn't the whole world exactly," she responded. The others laughed. Ron added that Jonathan might think he had the best wife but he, Ron, planned to hang on to his own wife a bit longer as she was making a good salary.

"You dog!" his wife exclaimed.

Larry, not to be outdone, proclaimed his wife Juliet was a champion tennis player and they were taking home awards almost every time they played doubles. "I'm not about to give that up."

Jonathan chuckled as he walked over to the shiny black grill and began cooking hamburgers. Sarah had set the picnic table earlier with a bright red plastic tablecloth, small American flags and glitter thrown everywhere. A stack of blue paper plates sat ready to be filled. A large bowl of potato chips sat in the middle of it all with ketchup and mustard nearby.

Larry, lifting his beer bottle high, made a toast: "Here's to our great country and freedom for all!"

"Hear, hear!" the well-heeled group chimed in as they upended their beers and took long swigs.

Later that evening, after the guests had gone, Jonathan and Sarah talked about what fun it had been. "We have some really good friends," Jonathan said, "The kind of people who'll always be there for us no matter what."

Sarah had her doubts.

"Yup," he continued. "We live well in this country. No wonder everyone wants to come to America."

"Except the visiting professor we met at Ron's party the other day," said Sarah. "He told me he has enjoyed his year of teaching in the states but is looking forward to getting home to the Netherlands."

"He must be missing his family. He ought to bring them over here too."

"I don't think that's it," she replied, "He said the government there treats people more fairly. If folks get sick or lose their jobs, they get help."

"Communism, by God! You want communism?"

"Well, no. But – but – is it really so bad for the government to help those in need?"

"If people were more careful, they wouldn't be in need," responded Jonathan.

"But for some, it seems much more difficult than for others. Like our house cleaner. She works really hard – so does her husband and, still, they don't make enough to pay their medical bills."

"They're black, for heaven's sake! What do you expect!" Sarah clenched her teeth but said nothing. Conversation ended. Later, wrapped in each other's arms, they made their way to the bedroom in their perfect ranch-style house with black shutters and a white picket fence located in an all-white suburb of Worcester, Massachusetts.

Monday morning rolled around, as it inevitably does, and Jonathan was up, dressed in a suit and drinking his coffee. Sarah, still in her bathrobe, had made scrambled eggs and was carefully scooping them on to his breakfast plate. She buttered the toast which had just popped up and set that down alongside the eggs. Then she grabbed a cup of coffee and settled at the small kitchen table across from her husband.

He looked up, set down his cup, reached across the table and laid his hand on hers. "You are so beautiful," he murmured, "especially first thing in the morning when you're just out of bed."

Sarah smiled, fully in love with this wonderful man. They had been married 8 months already but it felt like no more than a week, the time had flown by so quickly. Could she really be so lucky?

She was 20-years-old, living in her own apartment, working as a secretary at Madison Savings and Loan when both her parents had been killed in a car accident. After that, she had fallen in a deep black hole, felt she would never climb out again. She needed a ladder. That is when she met Jonathan. He provided one. Jonathan, an officer at Madison, had been compassionate, patient and caring. She owed him the world for rescuing her. He was a tall, handsome hunk, easy to love. He wanted to marry her. But she had a secret. If she told, she was afraid she would lose him forever. She didn't tell and now, here she was, living the good life but also living a lie.

Not long after Jonathan had left for work on Monday morning, the backdoor bell rang. The cleaning woman had arrived.

"Good morning, Laila, how are you today?" greeted Sarah.

"Fine, Mam. Glad it's cooled down a bit. Awful hot weekend."

"It certainly was," responded Sarah. "Did you all go to the parade?"

"No, guess we didn't. We don't really celebrate the 4th."

"You don't? I thought everyone did. Why don't you?"

"Well," and Laila pausing a moment before continuing, "It doesn't really celebrate *our* freedom. I mean, African-

American folks sort of got left behind when it came to that. Fact is, we're still struggling."

Sarah wasn't sure what to say. She smiled, then instinctively reached out to touch Laila's arm. Laila didn't look much older than Sarah herself but, coming from a different kind of home, Sarah felt a bit uncomfortable. "I'm sorry," was all she finally mumbled before taking her hand down and letting the cleaner get to work.

Sarah no longer worked. She had suffered frequent headaches. They had grown so frequent that she had trouble focusing on her job. She felt defeated.

"Then quit," Jonathan had said, "I make enough money to support us both. You're probably just stressed from the wedding and adjusting to your new life."

"I guess so," she replied though aware that was hardly the problem. The new life was exactly what she enjoyed. Staying home, she was able to work the headaches.

………………..

A few days after the 4th, Sarah woke up at dawn with considerable pain in her joints. She slid out of bed so as not to wake Jonathan, stumbled into the bathroom and took the last of several pain pills she had hidden in the closet behind a stack of towels. Back in bed again, she managed to fall back asleep until the alarm woke them both at seven.

She had tried her best not to let Jonathan see how badly she felt. After he had left for work, she collapsed in the easy chair. *Please, let this pain pass.* She knew she should go to a doctor but that would complicate her life. With her prescribed medication used up, she had tried controlling the pain with ibuprofen instead. She sat up to look down at her feet. They were indeed swollen. She had had these episodes before but they had always passed eventually. This one, however, did not.

When Jonathan returned from work that evening, she was in agony.

"I'm taking you to the ER right now," he insisted against her protests. "I can't bear to see you like this – got to find out what's going on." Sarah knew well enough but said nothing.

Jonathan drove her to the hospital where she was admitted to the ER, an IV line inserted and multiple tests carried out. Jonathan stayed by her side, holding her hand and wiping her warm brow, for now she was spiking a temperature.

Three hours later, test results back, a Doctor Sherman introduced himself to her, then pulled up a stool, sat down and was just ready to talk when Sarah beat him to it.

"Jonathan, could you maybe leave a minute and let me talk to the doctor in private?"

"Leave? I need to hear this as well as you. I want to know what's going on."

"I promise I'll tell you but I just want to be with the doctor right now."

"Okay," he said in a tone that showed it was not okay at all. However, he decided not to upset his wife at a time like this. "I'll be right outside. Call me if you need me," and he walked away, pulling closed the curtain circling her gurney.

Dr. Sherman looked her in the eye and said, "I think you already know what the problem is. It's a recurrence of your sickle cell anemia. I'm under the impression that your husband knows nothing about this. If that is the case, I think it's time you tell him. It's something you need to deal with together."

Suddenly the curtain was torn back and Jonathan rushed back into the room.

"Don't need to tell me? I heard what you just said. Sickle cell anemia? I thought that was something only blacks had."

"Have a seat please, said the doctor. It's clearly time we talk." Sarah's brown eyes opened wide with fright. She pulled the blanket up to her neck as if to fend off whatever was coming. Her dark curly hair straggled across the pillow. Her husband sat down in the plastic chair, took off his glasses, closed his eyes and pinched the bridge of his nose.

Silence filled the room until Jonathan finally opened his eyes and looked over at his wife. "How long," he asked in a slightly accusatory tone, "have you known about this?"

She answered in a subdued voice, almost too soft to hear. "It was diagnosed when I was a baby. Oh Jonathan, I thought I'd be okay. I didn't want to bother you with it at all."

"Bother me! I'm your husband. I need to know these things. But I didn't know whites got this as well. Are you sure of the diagnosis?"

"I am," replied the doctor.

"But how can she have it?" asked the distraught husband again.

"Maybe you can tell us," said Dr. Sherman in a kindly voice, turning to look at Sarah.

"God help me, I hoped it wouldn't come to this. I'm so sorry."

"Sorry for what?" her husband asked.

"Sorry for what I have to tell you."

"Well then, go ahead. Let's hear it," he demanded impatiently.

Sarah eyes began to fill up as she stuttered out her story. She had never told Jonathan she was adopted. All he had ever seen of her family was a photo of a middle-aged man dressed in a suit, standing stiffly beside a white woman sitting in a garden chair, a large straw hat shading her face, a lovely long dress down to her ankles. She had considered these parents her real ones for they had loved, provided and cared for her since she was a baby. She only found out about her biological parents when she grew older and learned that her recurring bouts of illness were caused by sickle cell anemia. At that time, she had been told that her real mother was African-American, her father of mixed blood. When Sarah was through speaking, she closed her eyes as if the weight of the world was too much to bear.

Dr. Sherman looked at Jonathan who exclaimed, "I've been blindsided! Good God! So, what do we do now?"

"I'll prescribe the medication she needs to hopefully get her out of this latest flare-up of her anemia. We'll give her two pills before she leaves. Then you can go but don't hesitate to come back if things get worse."

It was a silent drive home both of them looking at the road ahead. Neither saying anything. When they arrived, she dragged herself upstairs to fall into bed, sure it was the end of their marriage. *He has no tolerance for African-Americans, believes they are an inferior race. He will never accept me now.* She cried herself to sleep, soaking the pillow with tears. In one short day, the future had been yanked out from under her.

Later that night, she awoke and reached over to her husband's side of the bed. It was empty, just as she expected. Suddenly a small reading light in the far corner was switched on. Jonathan was sitting there in the rocking chair with a blanket over his knees.

"Feel any better?" he asked in a gentler voice than she expected.

"Yes, a little."

"Good."

She lay there, waiting for him to say something more but he was silent. Finally, she said, "You need to sleep. I can go down on the sofa. You can have the bed now."

He got slowly up, walked over to the bed and slid in beside her. She had turned on her side to swing her feet over the edge when he reached out and put his arm around her waist. "No, just stay."

The next morning, they were both up at seven. She fixed breakfast as usual. He drank his coffee as usual. There was little conversation.

"Take care of yourself," he said as he left.

"You too," she said, the tears welling up again. *So that was it – their final farewell.*

Sarah waited all day in a state of complete depression, walking aimlessly from one room to another while waiting for the phone call from Jonathan's lawyer. Once she stopped to look in the mirror: a young, slightly olive-skinned woman, slim, a broad face, full lips, appealing but not especially beautiful. Where would she go from here? Who would ever love her again? The stress of losing Jonathan was causing the pain to return. She found the new medicine, still sitting in a bag from the hospital pharmacy and swallowed two tabs as prescribed. She barely found the energy to put on her jeans and a top. *What's the point?* She thought. She didn't bother with lunch, having no appetite.

The phone never rang until Jonathan called at 5:30 to say he'd be late – nothing else, no explanation, no excuses – just late. *He didn't have time to talk to his lawyer from work so he's going over there now,* she reasoned. Not expecting him home for dinner, she had not prepared anything. Sarah turned on the evening news to distract herself but it didn't work. Her mind kept churning. She never heard a word the newscaster said.

At 8 o'clock, the door opened and Jonathan walked in. He took a long look at his disheveled wife, face mottled from crying, uncombed hair falling in her face. Then he looked away and said, "We have to talk. Let's sit down and try to straighten things out. I stopped for a couple of drinks on the way home. Needed some time to think. Didn't help much," he said, his eyes turning moist. "My head is pretty scrambled right now – trying to make sense of everything." *Even now, despite what has happened, she is still so special,* he reflected as he looked across the room at her.

Uncomfortable under his gaze, she got up and headed for the bathroom. "I'll be right back." She washed her face, combed her hair and straightened her clothes before returning to sit quietly down in the living room across from her husband. They stared awkwardly at each other before Jonathan finally put into words what they were both thinking. "What are we to do?"

"I don't know. I've made a mess of things. I'm so sorry."

"I guess it would have been better if you had been straight with me in the first place.'

"I do wish you had never found out."

"But you knew I would – eventually."

"I guess so. I just wanted you so much – still love you. Wish the race issue wasn't such a problem."

"Me too. Maybe if we don't tell anyone about your condition, we can keep it a secret."

"No, Jonathan. I can't do that anymore, can't live the lie. It's also a betrayal of my people."

"You really feel that way?" he asked, leaning forward to rest his arms on his knees.

"I do," she said, settling back deeper into the armchair as if to distance herself. "And that's where we are stuck. I'm going to have to leave, there's no other way."

"But, Sarah, I love you. That's not what I want."

"Maybe we just can't have what we want," she said, dissolving in sobs again.

"Look, let's give it a day or two. I need more time to think. Don't be going anywhere yet."

And so ended the evening. They slept that night spooned around each other.

In the morning, they said little. Jonathan left for work earlier than usual. His day did not go well, distracted as he was by thinking about his dilemma. It occurred to him that he didn't know anything about sickle cell anemia so, going online, he began to research it. What he read shocked him. It was far more serious than he had known. It also suddenly came to him that, until now, his concerns had been all about him, not about Sarah. *What a selfish oaf I am. She's the one who really has a problem, not me. She'll need a lot of support. I'm the best one to give it to her. I want to be there – need to forget about everything else.*

That evening, Jonathan arrived home a little earlier than usual. Sarah was polite but cool. *If I'm going to leave, it's better I start keeping my distance now,* she thought.

"Supper's ready, Jonathan." They sat down at the kitchen table. He tried to catch her eye but she would not look his way. How to reach out to her if she wouldn't give him a chance.

Just then, they heard barking coming from the yard. "What in the world?" Jonathan exclaimed.

They rushed to the back door where a short haired white and black dog was scratching at the screen. "Poor thing," sighed Sarah, "He must be lost."

Jonathan bent over the small trembling pup, stroking him under the chin. "He doesn't have a collar. Maybe he's a dump."

"What's that?"

"It's a dog whose owner doesn't want him anymore so he has to fend for himself."

"That's horrible."

"Agreed. An awful thing for anyone to do. I'll call the pound in the morning and see if someone's missing their dog."

"We really ought to bring him in the kitchen for the night so he'll be safe," suggested Sarah.

The dog padded inside, glad to find shelter. Sarah drew him a pan of water. Then she and Jonathan plunked down on the linoleum floor to pat and cuddle the pup.

"I didn't know you liked dogs?" he said.

"I love them – had one when I was little but it got hit by a car. I loved it so much. Broke my heart. Never wanted to risk losing one again so I didn't get another."

"If nobody claims this pup, would you take a chance on it?" Jonathan asked.

"Maybe."

"What I really meant to say was, should *we* take a chance on it?"

Sarah looked over at him. "*We*?" she said.

"Yes, *we*. I see a difficult road ahead but I want to travel it with you, no matter what." With that, he leaned over the dog, spilling the water bowl and causing the pup to jump up in alarm. He stretched and wrapped his arms around Sarah, giving her a big squeeze. Finally letting go, he picked up the puppy and set him in his lap, stroking his back to calm him down. "No need to be afraid in this home," he said, addressing the orphan dog, "Here, we'll take care of you, no matter where you're from."

Move Ahead

45

A loud bang followed by a deafening roar. A sheet of water slammed the windshield and swept over the car. Kit, the driver, turned to look at her cousin in the back who was gripping the seat with both hands, her eyes closed, her lovely pale face even paler.

"Belle, are you okay?" Kit shouted over the roar.

"I get claustrophobic. I'm terrified."

"You've never been through this before?"

"No," she replied. I'm a city girl, remember – never owned a car."

Rocky, a sturdy dark-haired woman sitting in the passenger seat, turned and reached back to lay a hand on Belle's trembling knee. "We'll be okay. It's almost over."

Just then, the noise abruptly stopped. Silence filled the void. Not for long. Another wave shook the car as it was entombed by a thick blue-green glop, sealing them into the darkened interior. The mess slid down the glass until a powerful gush of water blasted it away. Then a flashing red sign loomed up, with big red letters directing them to "Move ahead." Hot wind raked over the hood and along the sides of the car. Suddenly, they were outside again. Kit, steered them slowly forward into a new reality. When she and her friends had entered the car wash it was a cloudy February day in the North Country: brutally cold with mountains of snow everywhere. When they came out, it was summer.

"Oh my God! What just happened?" exclaimed Kit, a red-haired, broad-faced woman, as she applied the brakes and looked around. Rocky sat bolt upright, her mouth a gap of silent amazement.

Belle, slight of frame with golden hair, opened her eyes and merrily declared. "Wow! The sun is shining again. How wonderful."

But Kit, their intrepid driver, just sat in astonishment. Where was the road to the right leading up to Will Rogers Senior Residence? Where was Aldi's grocery store which should have been directly ahead of them? In fact, where were all the people? Her classmates, visiting from afar, were vaguely aware that something was the matter but it took them a minute to understand.

"How strange. This is your territory, surely you know where we are?" asked Rocky, finally finding her voice.

"I know we're not where I thought we were," replied Kit, "nor where we should be. I really don't recognize anything. And, that was the fastest change of seasons I've ever seen! It's not possible!"

"Apparently it is," responded Rocky, "because it happened."

"I declare, at least it's a change for the better," piped up Belle, "Roll down your windows sisters. Let's inhale the essence of this happy blessing."

The three women, not having seen one another for over 25 years, had gathered for a college reunion in Lake Placid. Belle and Rocky were staying at the Hotel Saranac. Kit, who lived in town, offered them a ride to the Conference Center where a lunch was to be held. Kit's husband Vince didn't mind his wife taking their car for the day but requested she first run it through the car wash on her way out of town. The SUV, caked in dried salt and sand, had turned from sleek black to mottled gray. The quick errand was not turning out as expected.

"I'll be damned! Where are we if we're not where we're supposed to be?" asked Rocky

"Personally, I don't care," responded Belle, "As long as I can see the sun again. Feel that warm air! Look at the beautiful wildflowers!"

Kit started to think she was hallucinating – like a drug trip in her college days. But she wasn't in college anymore and hadn't touched drugs in years. Was this a flashback? But how then could the others be having the same one? And Belle? She had never touched drugs anyway. Too afraid.

"Hey," said Rocky, "We can't just sit here. Another car will be coming out behind us. We're blocking the way. Kit looked in the rear-view mirror and discovered, to her shock, that the car wash was no longer there. Instead, a long road stretched all the way back to the horizon. Looking ahead, she saw the same: a country road lay like a ribbon straight through the landscape as far as she could see. White wooden fences on either side held back green meadows gently swaying with red and yellow flowers. The sky was brilliant blue. Distant hills lined the meadows. Sunshine brushed the scene in gold.

"Well," said Kit, "What should we do?"

"We can't just sit here," said Rocky, "That will get us nowhere. We need to move ahead."

"You agree, Belle?" asked Kit.

"If that's what you all think best, sure. Anyway, it's all so pretty – much better than Saranac Lake in February if you'll forgive me for saying so."

Kit remained quiet. She didn't agree with Belle's perception of winter. Kit loved the season: the dark conifers laden with snow, forest snuggled down under a blanket of white, the frosted trees, the occasional sight of glorious mountains crowned in pink as the rarely-seen sun dropped at the end of day … and skiing. If only everyone could know the delight of gliding through the woods, chickadees talking from branches overhead and multiple animal tracks, reminders that the wilderness belongs to all who live in it. However, Kit had learned her lesson long ago, best not to disagree on small matters.

Rocky broke the silence. "Where do you suppose this road goes to?"

"Who knows?" answered Kit, "But now that summer has arrived, the driving should be easy. Shall we follow it and see where we end up?"

"I'm in," twittered Belle from the back seat, letting out a high-pitched giggle.

"Sure, why not?" agreed Rocky.

And off they went driving slowly along a very smooth one-lane road, too narrow to turn around and go back. After 10 minutes, Kit announced that she was going to pull over for a moment and call Vince and let him know what happened to them. Leaning over to grab her handbag from the floor where it lay by Rocky's feet, she noticed her shoes.

"Hey," she said, "How come you wore sandals to go out in the snow?"

"What are you talking about?" responded Rocky before looking down to see that her feet were indeed tucked inside a nice pair of brown leather summer shoes. Words failed her again.

"Are we dreaming, all of us?" wondered Kit. She grabbed her phone only to discover: no bars.

"No bars?" repeated Belle, the city girl. "I never heard of 'no bars'. Now that's scary."

"It'll be a lot more scary if there are no real bars along here," quipped Rocky. With that, they spotted the first signs of habitation: "The Raccoon Saloon, ladies welcome."

"Oh look, there's one now. Let's stop and go in. I could use a drink and maybe someone can explain what's going on."

"Are you kidding," shrieked Belle. "Go in without a man? Never. You all go if you want but I'm staying right here in the car."

"Come on," said Rocky, "What are you afraid of?"

"Men!"

"You? The honey that always had the male bees buzzing?" replied Rocky, "and still does, no doubt –

probably why you never married, having too much fun to settle down.”

“Well, I do like fun,” giggled Belle, “but with men I know something about. Here, what kind of men would hang out in a place like this? Certainly nobody I want to mix with!”

“We’re just going to go meet a few folks, maybe women as well,” said Kit. “We’re not planning to sleep with them. Because you don’t know them doesn’t mean they’re bad.” Kit realized she was being unusually confrontational but Belle, in her eyes, was showing blatant prejudice. “How are we going to know what’s going on if we don’t go in and ask?”

“Okay, okay, I get your point but I still don’t want to stop here. You know, I’ve never told anyone this before but sometimes my dad really got into alcohol and when he did, things got rough at home. I don’t trust guys in bars.”

“Sure,” said Kit, “Sorry. I didn’t know. Let’s not make any decision unless we all agree on it.”

“No problem,” added Rocky, “but beautiful as this all is, we need to figure out what’s going on.” And so, they passed The Raccoon Saloon, to follow the road ahead. It continued as lovely as before but after a while, they noticed that the scenery never changed: same mountains, same fences, same meadows full of flowers. Belle kept exclaiming over the scenery and the warm air pouring in the windows. Rocky said she’d welcome a little variety. Kit didn’t say much at all until, looking at the gas gauge, she realized they were almost on empty.

“We need a filling station soon or we’re going to get stranded.” Just then, up ahead, they spotted a sign for Mobil. “Wow, just in time.” They pulled in and, feeling the need for a break, stepped out of the car. Rocky, being a single gal and used to doing things for herself, grabbed the pump and gas started gurgling into the empty tank. Kit looked over at Belle and exclaimed, "What a beautiful summer dress!"

"Dress? This isn't *my* dress! Where'd this come from? I put on snow pants this morning to ward off your frigid climate. I remember thinking the other alumnae would be shocked when they saw me looking like that. A dress? Not that I mind. It's character that counts not looks," she said as she pulled out a tiny mirror, inspected her face and carefully applied lipstick to her dainty mouth.

Rocky went inside to pay. An old man in greasy coveralls was behind the counter. "Could you tell me where this road leads?" she asked.

"Couldn't say. Never been to the end. No rush to get there either. Where is it you're headed?"

"Well," now that you ask, I don't really know where we're headed. However, it's getting pretty monotonous just driving this straight and narrow road. Are there any turnoffs?"

"Sure," they're plenty but you have to watch carefully for them. They aren't always obvious."

With that, the three women climbed back in the car but not without first inspecting each other and realizing they were suddenly all dressed for summer. Rocky, the practical one, had on khaki shorts with lots of pockets and a light wick-away-the sweat tee shirt. Belle, wearing a sleeveless pink silk dress, hemline above the knee, looked quite sexy. Kit, not one for dressing up, wore black pants with a blue plaid cotton long sleeved shirt. They were perplexed yet gratified with their new clothes.

Earlier, when driving along they had been lulled into a kind of trance. Now, they sat up and made a point of looking for side roads. It was not long before one appeared branching off to the right. A high brick wall ran along its side. "That looks way too ominous to me," said Belle, "look how it cuts the view on that side of the road. I prefer to see what's around me."

"Not ominous to me," said Kit. "I grew up in Dannemora, a town with a prison right in the middle of it. The tall wall meant protection from the inmates. Walls make me feel safe."

"Yes, but what about walls that lock out people, like the Berlin Wall once did, and the wall across our Southern states? High solid walls mean exclusion, prejudice and discrimination. I don't like them," said Rocky.

"Oh, but then there is poet Robert Frost insisting that 'fences make good neighbors.'" added Kit.

"That's so too," agreed Rocky, "low stone walls like the ones on farm land in New England – full of cool things – lichens, mosses, fossils, snakes and..."

"Snakes!" shrieked Belle. "What's so cool about snakes?"

"So, what should I do, take the road or not?" asked Kit

"No," declared Belle. And so, having agreed all decisions had to be unanimous, they continued on.

Another turnoff appeared, this time on the left side. Kit slowed. They looked down the new road and saw it was lined with tall buildings, some even skyscrapers. Lit up show rooms cast yellow light on the sidewalks.

"Aah! Now that's my kind of place," exclaimed Belle, "Should be lots of shopping, concerts and museums. Let's go."

"Your kind, not mine," responded Rocky. "Too crowded, too confining – no fresh air. Entertainment I don't need, thank you. I can make my own."

"Well, aren't you just the old New England puritan! You miss a lot of good times with an attitude like that," quipped Belle.

They kept on driving, soon spotting the turnoff which led toward a river.

"Shall we try it?" asked Kit. "Rivers are always interesting." She headed the car down the new road only to find it dead-ended at the shore. The river coursed its way through lush green forests with great trees leaning over the sun-dappled water. There, on a sandy beach a dinghy awaited.

"Great!" said Rocky. "We can finally get out of the car and explore by boat. What fun."

"For you, maybe, but not for me. I can't swim," complained Belle. "Besides, it could be dangerous out there all by ourselves."

"By ourselves? A lot safer than in the city where you have to worry about pickpockets and muggers. 'In wildness is the preservation of the world,' as Thoreau once wrote."

"That maybe so," said Belle, "but I'd rather preserve cities." They turned around and went back to the main road.

"Listen," said Kit, after a half-hour more of cruising through the lovely countryside, "I'm getting hungry. What are we going to do for food and bathrooms?" Immediately they spotted a food take out stop to their right and pulled over. There was a window and a gray-haired woman in a white apron standing at the counter to take orders.

"What do you have?" asked belle.

"Anything you want." They found that hard to believe but indeed, whatever they ordered, it was cooked up and delivered to them in minutes. They sat outside at a nicely finished picnic table. After eating, they found clean port-a-potties in the back.

"Could you tell us where we are?" Rocky asked the woman in the window.

"Right here." she answered.

"I mean," where does this road lead?"

"That depends on where you want to go? Only you know that."

"I think we want to go back to where we started," said Kit.

"I'd be careful. You might just get what you wish for –
miss a lot of adventure that way," the woman replied as she
began to fade, along with the food stand, the table and port
a-potties.

The friends piled back in the car. What did it all mean?
A lively conversation ensued.

"I don't know about you but I'm ready to skip the
adventure and just go back," said Belle. She began to
quietly sniffle before breaking down into full-blown sobs.
"I don't like any of this at all."

Rocky turned around and handed Belle a handkerchief.
"Don't worry," she said gently, "We'll figure this out but
we have to ask ourselves what 'going back' really means?
Did the woman mean going back to birth or back to our
college years or back to Saranac Lake?"

"All I know is that she said to be careful what we wish
for," responded Kit. "By the way, have you noticed that
every time we need something like gas or food, it appears?
It's all very easy but we're getting nowhere. The scenery
never changes, the road never curves, the sky stays
perpetually blue."

"As for me," exclaimed Rocky, turning back to study the
road, "I like a good storm now and then. It's just all blue
sky. Maybe we're missing out by never taking the chance
on a turnoff."

"I know what I want," said Belle. "A car wash! Maybe
that way we can drive through and come out where we
started from."

"I'm not so sure, Belle, we don't know if we will come
out at the same place again," responded Kit. "This is so
magical. I, for one, am beginning to enjoy it. Let's take the
next turnoff no matter what."

"Oh no," moaned Belle as she huddled in the back seat
and more tears flowed down her lovely cheeks. "All I want
is to stop this crazy trip and get back to normal. Life wasn't
so bad."

"True," said Rocky, "but life's short. Why not experience something new before falling into our graves?"

Kit remained silent. She liked to go along with everyone but it was clear that would not be possible. There comes a time, she realized, when you finally have to pick sides and take a stand.

"Tell you what. Why don't we wish for another car wash?"

With that, a road suddenly veered off to the right, and there one stood, along with a second car.

"There you go, Belle. We're at a new juncture. You dare take that car through the car wash?"

Belle sat up in the back seat, wiped her eyes and stared.

"All alone? You all aren't coming with me?"

"No, my friend, we're not even sure it will take you back to the same place. Anyway, we are way too curious about what lies ahead. However, this is your chance if you want to go."

"My goodness! All by myself? … okay, I'll do it," Belle opened the door and stepped out, looking lovely but vulnerable in her summer dress. Kit and Rocky got out too. They hugged each other, held on a little longer than usual, smiled through their tears, then sent her off.

"Good luck!" And away she drove, her arm jingling with bracelets waving goodbye out the car window.

"You think she made the right decision?" asked Kit.

"Who knows what the right decision is? I must say, though, she showed tremendous courage taking off by herself like that. So, unlike the Belle I thought I knew. I misjudged her."

Rocky and Kit got back in the car and sat for a moment before setting out again, Rocky behind the wheel.

"I'm curious," said Kit, "why you're willing to keep on going like this?"

Rocky paused to think before answering, "Because magic may only happen once in a lifetime. I'd be a fool not to embrace it while I can. I'm ready to leave the main road, turnoff, take a chance. I'd gotten into a rut at home: work, sleep, work, sleep. I remember my mother named me Rocky after those low stone walls back in New England. She said they were sturdy, strong and seemed to explore the woods and fields the way she hoped I would. The moment has come. I'm ready to move ahead. What about you?"

"I'm not sure," replied Kit, "I have a happy life but I'm a writer – looking for new inspiration – up for adventure. I figure when we've had enough, we can always try the car wash again."

The two women looked at each other, laughed, then raised their drinks in a toast, for suddenly they were each holding a champagne glass. At the same moment, they both exclaimed,

"Let's move ahead. Here's to the wild side of life!"

Hurricane Joe

Hurricane Joe got hauled away by the deputies. He had assaulted a visitor at his cabin. "Two years!" the judge declared, "That should teach you to stay sober!" But Hurricane Joe already knew about sober. That's why he had built himself a small log cabin way back in the woods, away from bars, his fellow man and temptation. There he had lived peacefully for several years, the farm worker up the road dropping off groceries from time to time. The rest of his needs were met by a small garden tilled out back, and by hunting deer and squirrels. He was a good man when sober, a hurricane when drunk. The visitor, dismissive of his host's problem, had arrived with a couple of Jack Daniels bottles. That was all it took. The two men had fallen into an argument and Joe had lost control.

His cabin now abandoned, chinks of moss dropped from between the logs, the door frame was warped, a broken window let in the rain, the stove pipe tilted to one side. Word went out that it was haunted. A group of boys had hiked out the long path leading to the cabin in order to ransack the place. It didn't happen. Moaning came from inside. They beat a fast retreat. Occasionally hikers would happen on the place. They didn't stick around either. The moaning drove them away.

"A bad soul," they said. "Just like Hurricane Joe. Best keep your distance." And so, they did. The cabin sat slowly falling apart. One day, Gypsy Sal and her daughter, eight-year-old Minka, were in town to pick up groceries. They came upon a group of boys on the street corner. The boys hadn't seen them coming or they would have backed away in terror for Gypsy Sal was said to be a witch. As Minka and her mother came closer, they overheard the boys talking about a terrifying ghost at Hurricane Joe's place, how they were going out there to steal his stuff but a ghost had chased them away.

Now Minka had grown up with a mother who told fortunes, read people's palms and communicated with the dead. She didn't think ghosts were scary at all; they were just people trying to return to earth again. She and her mother lived at some distance from the village in a small trailer on a vacant lot. Townspeople, especially the women, some married, some not, would visit her in secret to find out who their husbands were sleeping with, or how to snare a rich guy, or how to get rid of warts. But nobody ever admitted to visiting her as she was different from "normal" people and thus an outcast. However, enough were willing to pay for her services, to keep Gypsy Sal and her daughter more or less provided for.

Minka had a rather lonely life, living as she did with a witch. But the witch loved her dearly and did what she could to protect her child from the bullies in town. Minka grew up playing in the woods, making friends with rabbits and snakes and birds. The woods were where she felt safe. So, when she heard about Hurricane Joe's cabin, she became curious, as children often are before it is pounded out of them in school. Minka didn't go to school like other kids. She was taught at home and so continued to be quite curious.

One day, she decided to go look for Hurricane Joe's cabin. It was a long walk but she had a general idea where it was located. She finally found the rough trail to his place. It was overgrown and hard to follow but she was a good tracker and eventually made her way to the cabin, which sat on the far side of a small clearing. As she approached, she heard a plaintive sound like moaning. "Poor soul," she thought, "it must be a spirit trapped inside."

She climbed a couple of rotting steps and pushed open the creaky door. It was darker inside than she had expected. It took a minute for her eyes to adjust. Suddenly, something exploded out of the corner and flapped past, brushing her face with its wings and disappearing through the broken window. "An owl! So that's what the moaning was," she exclaimed out loud. "Don't be afraid Mr. Owl. I'll be your friend," she called after it.

As her eyes adjusted, she began to look about. It was a perfect one-room playhouse: a cot in the corner with a raggedy woolen blanket, a wobbly wooden table and two rickety chairs, an old rusty stove, and even jackets, shirts and pants still hanging on pegs. On shelves nailed to the walls, she found pans, dishware, forks and knives. Her brown eyes opened wide in delight and she danced a little jig right there on the wide-board floor, her black pigtails flying as she spun around and around, her feet kicking up a plume of dust. Growing warm, she removed her patchwork coat and hung it on an unused peg. Then she plopped herself down on one of the rickety chairs and gazed around at the cabin's interior. In her rainbow-colored dress, she brightened the room. A few minutes later, she looked up to see the owl sitting on a branch outside the window. "It's okay," she called out, "You can come back in. I don't mind sharing." But the owl, just sat there staring. Then she heard scratching noises from a tiny hole in the corner of the room. Tiptoeing over, to see what it could be, she saw a gray mouse chewing on an old towel. "Well mouse, you must be building a nest. "I can help," she said, "I'll bring some cotton tomorrow. It will be nice and soft for your babies."

Maybe it's better if owl doesn't live inside anymore. He might eat my little friend, she realized. I'll *make him a good place to live nearby.* Now it was getting late, the sun was sliding down toward the hills. Time for her to head home. She skipped down the path, filled with happiness as only an innocent child can be after a new discovery.

When Minka arrived for supper, she was so excited about her adventure that she couldn't stop talking. "Mother, I need a broom to clean up the floor. It's so dusty." There were plenty of brooms in the trailer, not because Gypsy Sal was a witch but because she kept a very clean home. "Don't tell anyone about the cabin, Mother. I want it to be our very own secret." Of course, there was really no one Gypsy Sal could have told because she had no real friends.

"Just be careful, my sweet, someday Hurricane Joe will return. It's his cabin and he may not like anyone else disturbing it."

"I'm not disturbing it, I'm just making it better for when he comes home," replied Minka. "I feel sorry for him. That mean visitor never should have let him drink."

....

The next day, Minka returned to the cabin, this time carrying a broom and a pocket full of cotton. Mr. Owl had moved outside but sat nearby in a tree watching. Minka went to work, cleaning and putting everything in order. She also emptied her pocket and laid the cotton down in one corner for the resident mouse. She loved animals and they loved her back. She was glad to have their company in the little house. She covered the broken window with a piece of tin found lying out back, left over from constructing the roof. No more rain leaking in. Then she went outside and dug up moss to stuff back between the logs and keep out the wind.

While looking for moss, she discovered an old hand pump nearby. It was too heavy for her to work so she asked her mother to come help her get it going. Gypsy Sal went out the next day, poured water down the pump, worked the handle up and down priming it, and soon water was pouring out the spout. Minka clapped her hands in joy.

"Now I can wash the dishes and pans and give the birds and animals water," she exclaimed.

Then she showed her mother around the cabin.

"It's a lovely spot, but don't forget, someday you'll have to leave."

"I know," replied the elfin child, "Poor man. I'm going to keep it real nice for him so folks won't think it's abandoned and try to wreck everything."

Suddenly her mother had a vision of the gang of boys finding her daughter there alone. She didn't like it. That evening, after their supper of gruel and berries, she sat her daughter down for a talk.

"Minka, do you know anything about crows?"

"They fly around a lot. They're always talking."

"So, you know there are lots of them. Crows are very special. They're like spirits of the dead. They see everything. That's why they're so smart. When you go to the cabin tomorrow, take a handful of corn and see if you can lure them out of the sky down to the cabin."

And that is what Minka did. Every day after that, she would bring corn with her and call to the crows to come eat. Slowly, they began to respond, flapping down to the ground to feast. Becoming tamer and tamer, they were soon eating out of her hand. Mr. Owl, up in the tree, was not fond of crows and would disappear when he heard them coming, for crows love to harass owls and he wanted nothing to do with that. Minka noticed and planned to make a special home for the owl, but she didn't know how to do it. The problem was solved one day, when just as the crows were arriving, she looked up to see the owl disappear into a hole in the trunk of a big old tree. "Oh good," she said to him. "You found a safe place for yourself."

Meanwhile, Gypsy Sal had work to do. She knew how important the cabin had become to her daughter and what happiness she found playing there all day. It was important to protect her. So, from that time on, each time one of the towns people came to her for help, she managed to mention crows. "Crows are spirits of the dead and sacred. Woe to anyone who tries to harm a crow. If they do, sickness and death will follow," she would tell one woman. Or, to someone else she would let slip that "Crows defend the innocent, throw curses on bad people, attack with their sharp beaks, draw blood and shoot poison into their bodies."

Word about the crows spread through town. Nobody knew where the notion started because no one would admit to visiting Gypsy Sal.

………………..

Over the next several weeks, little by little, the cabin took on new life. Minka went every day to clean and play and talk to her animal friends. The weeks turned to months until one day, when Minka had just arrived and gone inside, she heard a noise coming from the edge of the clearing. She stepped out again to see what it was when a stone whizzed by her head, hitting the door behind her.

"Witch girl! Weirdo! Afraid of school. We'll show you!" screamed several voices from the woods. Another stone winged by her as she ducked.

"Help, help," she cried, bolting back inside and slamming the door, "Get away from here!"

"Devil girl! We're coming to burn you out," and one of the boys who had been hiding in the woods, started running across the clearing carrying a can of gas.

"I'm not a devil," screamed Minka, "Help, somebody help me!" Just then the sky grew darker as the crows, looking for their morning snack, began to gather.

"Hey, look at all those crows!" cried someone.

"Look out, they're coming down!" yelled another.

By this time, the boys had left the protection of the woods to join their leader who was out in the open. The crows, perhaps sensing something wrong, were soon flapping and cawing around their heads.

"They're attacking!" cried a third. Their mothers had recently been telling them frightening things about crows. Horrified, they waved their arms over their heads to fend them off. One of the crows flew right at the boy with the gas can. Was the crow looking for food or attacking? The boy had heard that the stories about how crows could poison people. He shook in terror, dropped the can and ran the other way, the rest of the boys right along with him, all jabbering and crying.

Minka looked on in wonder. "Good crows," she cried out when the boys were gone, "You saved me," and she emptied her pockets of corn and threw it on the ground where the crows awaited their usual breakfast.

That night, she told her mother what had happened. "Oh, my darling," said Gypsy Sal, "It worked.

"What worked?" asked her daughter.

"I've been busy spreading tales about the power of crows."

"And people believed you?"

"They did. Folks around here are superstitious. They'll fall for anything they hear. I knew they'd go for this one."

"You mean you don't really think crows are smart? You don't really believe they're the spirits of the dead?"

"They're smart alright. I don't know about the rest," replied her mother. "I just can't be sure. What I do know is that people are pretty gullible. They'll latch onto anything they hear. That's why I can make a living telling fortunes. It also helps me keep you safe. That's what matters the most," she said as she gathered her lovely black-haired daughter onto her lap to cuddle her as any mother would.

The very next day, Minka was back at the cabin, certain she would be protected by the crows. However, no sooner was she in the door than she again heard a noise outside. This time she stayed inside and peaked out the window. There in the clearing stood an old man in raggedy pants and a red plaid jacket. He was staring at the cabin while stroking a friendly crow sitting on his shoulder. A big smile splashed across Minka's face as she ran out the door to welcome Hurricane Joe to his home.

Roscoe's Way

Zelda first noticed him at her exhibition. He had stood still for several minutes, staring at her favorite painting hanging at the far end of the room. Well-wishers had crowded around her and she had lost sight of him. Thanks to an abundance of gallery crawlers, all liberally supplied with wine, she had been occupied with both conversation and sales. Afterwards, more than happy with the results, she was nevertheless sorry not to have had a chance to talk with the stranger at the end of the room. The memory of him stayed with her long after the evening was over. He had stood out among the cocktail crowd. She had only seen him from the back: straight dark shoulder-length hair, a red flannel shirt neatly tucked into crisp jeans. *Who was he?*

She did not see him again until several weeks later at the farmers' market. She was reaching for a lovely red juicy tomato when someone else snatched it first. Startled, she looked up to see the mystery man from the gallery.

"Did you want this?" he asked, smiling at her.

"Well, I did, that's why I was reaching for it."

"Here," he said, holding it out on his hand. "The only thing I really want is a chance to say hello."

"Hello," she responded.

"Hi, I'm Roscoe Reynolds, I live just outside the village. I attended your art show opening and was very impressed with your paintings."

"Yes, I did see you there. I'm glad you enjoyed the show."

"I did. I'd love to buy one of your paintings but there's no more room on my walls. I'm a collector of sorts and there is simply no space left for anything else."

I've heard that one before, Zelda thought to herself. Nevertheless, he was a good-looking guy, slender, about 50 she guessed, clean shaven, high cheekbones, straight nose and a pleasantly crooked mouth.

"Sure, no problem," she replied, "How come I've never seen you around before? Are you a newcomer?"

"You might say that. I've been here 8 years and that pegs me as a newbie in these parts."

"Still, I would have thought in a small village like this I'd have run into you before."

"I stay close to home. I live at the end of a long dirt road. It's pretty isolated. It suits me most of the time. I have my friends on zoom and email. It seemed to be enough until I saw your work. You know, I felt a real connection to your paintings. I'd love to see more of them."

"If you really felt that way, why didn't you talk to me at the opening?"

"I guess that's not my scene. It felt too crowded. However, if you have time, I wonder if you'd let me buy you a coffee now. We could sit at one of those picnic tables over there."

So, what is the harm in that? Zelda asked herself. *We're in a public place with lots of people nearby and this guy is intriguing.* They found an empty table at the edge of the park, not far from the market, and sat down opposite one another.

Zelda was lonely but after losing her husband Jake, she had never met anyone who could match up to him. He, a gifted college professor with a drinking problem, had died long ago, leaving her to raise their kids alone. Early in the marriage, he had hit and injured a pedestrian when he was driving home from a meeting. He had received a heavy fine, a suspended license and was required to sign into a rehab program. He was compliant, even got his drinking under control, but soon after that, he himself was hit and killed by a drunk driver. Now, years later, the kids having moved away for work, she was on her own, still living off Jake's life insurance and whatever else she could earn selling her paintings.

Roscoe and Zelda connected at once, discussing the long-standing subject of what defines a creation as art and what place art has in culture.

"A good painting gives the viewer different insights into reality," Zelda commented.

"I agree, and many other kinds of art do the same," he replied as he lifted his coffee for a sip, all the while watching her over the rim of his cup.

"Like, what kinds?"

"Well, take writing for instance. Nonfiction is like the account of a journalist. It takes skill to do it well but is, after all, just a report of facts. Fiction, however, like a painting, is a magic mirror reflecting the truth behind the facts. It reveals the wonder of life.

"I never thought about it quite like that." Zelda replied, leaning forward as if she didn't want to miss a word of what Roscoe was saying. "Do you read a lot of fiction?"

"Every chance I get when I'm not otherwise occupied."

"And how are you otherwise occupied?" she asked, forgetting about her own coffee, entranced as she was by Roscoe.

"I have an online job, keeps me glued to the computer a good part of the day."

And that is how it all started. Zelda had many local friends and a car. Roscoe had no local friends and no car. "Too expensive and contributes to climate change. As long as I can, I'll stick to my bike. However, unfortunately, it is not a bicycle built for two."

Under Zelda's influence, Roscoe began to get out more. He would bike into the village, often meeting her at the library for a lecture or at the Sun Ray Café for lunch.

Sometimes they would take in a concert on the green. If it was going to be dark before returning home, she would pick him up in her car at the end of the road to his place. "I don't maintain the dirt road anymore and it's become undriveable," he told her.

Zelda introduced him to her friends. They were impressed by his quiet manner but obvious brilliance. "Lucky you," her best friend Sally said, "to find a guy like that."

Roscoe often recommended good books to her. Zelda, for her part, invited him on trips to distant museums with contemporary exhibits, explaining the value she saw in some of the more radical paintings. The friendship progressed to more than that. Roscoe often spent the night at her place.

Occasionally Zelda looked in the mirror (which was not magical) and tried to see what he saw in her, a 48-year-old, slightly overweight woman with gray hair in long braids. Her face was beginning to crease, her lips losing their fullness. It was a miracle that he wanted to be with her. He was in good shape and, as he told her, took long hikes, chopped wood to fill his stove, and did all his own house repairs. However, something still didn't add up. She wasn't sure just what it was he did on his computer all day.

"You know so much about me," she said one day, "but I still don't know why it is that you moved here, what your life was before this and what you do for a living."

"Ah," he said, "Fair enough. It's time I explain. I was married at a young age. It didn't work. My wife left. No kids. I've been on my own ever since. But there's more. I will tell you but you must swear not to tell anyone else."

Zelda suddenly got nervous: *why did his wife leave him and what could be so terrible that no one must know?*

"Not tell anyone? Is this something bad?"

"No. It's just this. I'm actually a writer, that's why I'm on the computer so much. Several of my books have won awards and I've been nominated for the National Book Award."

"That's amazing! But…I guess I'm really ignorant because I've never heard of your books."

"That's because I write under a pen name. Have you heard of Gordon Harrington?"

"Gordon Harrington! My God. Is that you?"

"Yes. And now, you must never breathe a word of it to anyone."

"But why?"

"Because where I lived before, everyone knew who I was. Not only neighbors but the media were constantly after me. It got to be a circus. Not the way I wanted to live at all. I couldn't continue writing with the constant interruptions. Living in solitude leaves me free of societal expectations. It is the ultimate crazy way to enjoy my life to its fullest."

Gordon Harrington! Hard to believe! On the other hand, it made sense. He was well educated with a deep knowledge of literature and a sharp mind. But, not to tell anyone? How I would love to. It's going to be hard to keep it all to myself but I'm happy to have such a secret.

After that revelation, Roscoe seemed to grow more relaxed, often sharing with her the struggles he endured as a writer. This encouraged her to open up more as well. She told him about the difficulty of persevering in painting the world as she saw it instead of dropping her standards and appealing to the commercial market. "People consider my paintings strange. They don't understand them. I need to sell but hate caving in to painting the ordinary. Wish I had the same courage with other things as I have with my paintings. I live such a conventional life."

Her friends began to notice a change in Zelda. She was more upbeat, less moody. "No wonder," they commented, "with a catch like that guy."

They wanted to know everything about him, including where he lived. When she told them, one friend responded, "Oh, that's the Robertson place," referring to the previous owner as is customary until the present owner lives there no longer. "My dad used to go over and help Mr. Robertson split wood. I don't know that anyone has seen the place in years. It used to be pretty run down. What's it like now?"

"I don't know. I've never seen it but I do know that Roscoe lives there off the grid and does all his own repairs. He's handy with a hammer and saw."

"You've never been out there? You spend all that time together but haven't seen his house? That's strange."

"Not really, he tells me the road is not drivable so I pick him up at the end of it or he rides his bike into the village and I meet him there." Of course, he had also told her it was his escape place for writing. He wanted to keep it that way. However, she couldn't tell that secret so she said nothing more.

Zelda had told her friends that it all seemed too good to be true. "Life just doesn't go like this."

"Nonsense," Sally replied, "Yours does. Keep the faith." She was to remember those words later.

A few days later, Zelda had arranged to pick Roscoe up at the end of his road so they could attend a chamber music concert at the Unitarian Church. She arrived but he did not. Usually punctual, he had often spoken of the selfishness of people who are late and keep others waiting. Yet, here she was, waiting. When 15 minutes had passed, she grew annoyed. When a half-hour passed, annoyance turned to worry. After 45 minutes, she decided to get out of the car and go see what had happened. After all, he lived alone way out there in the woods. If he had had an accident, nobody would know.

It was growing dark as she walked along the dirt road to his place, one in much better condition than she had expected. She had gone a quarter of a mile before she spotted a roof, then a front porch. But there she stopped abruptly. The porch was heaped with bulging black garbage bags, a Volvo without tires sat on cement blocks in the side yard, various pieces of equipment were lying outside every which way around the house: a log splitter, a table saw, a metal trailer streaked with rust and a number of other things she couldn't identify, including bulky items wrapped in blue tarpaulins. It was a creepy looking place with all the stuff filling the yard and porch. Even the windows were blocked on the inside by furniture. Old window boxes, a fallen down chicken coop and rolled up fencing added to the clutter.

Zelda stood stock still, a feeling of dread creeping over her. *Could this really be his house?* she wondered. It clearly was as the road ended there. Zelda turned and fled, her shoes pounding the road, her breath coming in gasps. *I need help. I don't dare go closer by myself. It's too weird.* When she was safely back in the car, she waited a moment to calm down before dialing Sally.

"Sally," she said, "I'm out at Roscoe's place but I need help. I'm afraid something might have happened. I don't dare go check on him by myself. Being as your husband is an EMT, do you think he could meet me out here and go with me?"

"Of course, he will, but what's going on?"

"I don't exactly know but Roscoe didn't meet me at the end of the road as he always does. I need Travis to go with me and see what's going on."

Travis arrived 20 minutes later, emergency bag in hand. He and Zelda hurried up the road until they came in sight of the house. "Whoa," Travis exclaimed in shock, "What a mess. Okay, guess we better get inside and look for him." They climbed the wooden stairs, stepped around the bags and knocked. No answer.

"Okay, let's try the door." The door opened into a gloomy interior filled to the ceiling with boxes, tables, desks, chairs and shelves full of books. There were more books on the floor, along with magazines and newspapers. Multiple framed pictures were leaning one on the other against a cupboard. Zelda was spooked by quiet rustling noises until she realized it was cats, lots of them, slinking over the top of all the stuff.

"Hello, hello!" Travis called out. They heard a faint response.

"Down here, I'm in the basement." Fear and worry gripped Zelda. She could hardly breathe. *What was going on?*

"We're coming," replied Travis, undaunted, "how do we get there?"

"In the kitchen. You'll see the steps," came the distant reply.

They made their way through narrow corridors of stuff towering over their heads and eventually came to what they supposed was the kitchen. There was no visible stove or sink, just piles of dishes and pans covering everything. In the corner was a refrigerator with a couple of dead plants on top. They found the doorway to the steps. Travis felt along the wall for a light switch, found it and turned it on. Stairs leading to the basement were piled on both sides with everything from mouse traps to flower pots.

"Careful," warned Roscoe, "careful on the steps. I tripped coming down them. I think my leg is broken." There he lay on the basement floor, neatly dressed in a long-sleeved shirt and freshly pressed jeans. He was obviously in considerable pain. "You're here. Thank God! I'm so sorry about all this."

It didn't take long for Travis to confirm that the leg was indeed broken. He had an air splint in his bag and applied it at once, providing some relief. Zelda stood back, appalled and confused by the whole scene. It didn't make sense.

"I'm calling an ambulance," declared Travis. "Got to get you to a hospital." Roscoe kept apologizing for the trouble he had caused. He looked over at Zelda but she wouldn't look back at him. *This is my Roscoe? The man I thought I knew so well He's tricked me. He might not be Gordon Harrington either,* she thought.

In addition to the broken leg, it turned out that Roscoe had a broken rib which had punctured his lung. This necessitated putting in a chest tube and admitting him to the hospital. Zelda was in a state of despair. She had loved this man so much but now was learning things that were strange and hard to process. He had lied about his pen name and lived in a dump. Who was he really?

The second day after his accident, she decided she would visit and have it out with him. When she arrived at his hospital room, a strange man was sitting by Roscoe's bed. *This is going to be awkward* she thought, as she knocked on the partially open door to get the attention of the two men.

"Is it alright to come in?" she asked.

"Zelda my love. I'm so happy you came. I have a lot of explaining to do but first, meet my editor Sam from Gibraltar Publishing." Sam was dressed in wool slacks, a tweed jacket, bow tie and white shirt. He stood up to shake hands, clearly a city man out of place.

"How do you do, Zelda. I heard about Gordon's accident and came from New York to cheer him up with some good news. His next book is coming out in November."

"Oh!" she gasped, "Oh, that's really nice. Congratulations," she said turning in surprise to smile in Roscoe's direction. Then she looked over at Sam, "Nice to meet you, please sit down. I just stopped to say hi."

"No, no. You take this seat, I was on my way out," he said, pointing to the chair, "Glad I have the pleasure of meeting you."

Once his editor had left, Roscoe began, "I'm so sorry about all this. Thank you again for rescuing me." After a pause, he continued, "I should have told you about my house earlier but I was afraid of losing you if you knew. People have accused me of being a hoarder. I just call it storing up memories. That's why I live where I do. Nobody comes creeping around complaining about my home and telling me I need counseling. Can you understand that?"

"I don't know. It just seems so... so... so... I don't really know what to say."

"Then don't say anything but please don't leave me."

But Zelda stayed only a few minutes, at a loss how to go on from there. When she arrived home, she immediately went to her computer and looked up hoarding. It was an addiction, she learned, something not easily changed. Holding on to stuff, not throwing anything away was an expression of insecurity. She was saddened by what she read. He had seemed so wonderful but she realized she hadn't really known the whole man before. At least he had not lied, he was indeed Gordon Harrington. But, now that she knew the real man, what should she do? It would be all over the village, the story of Roscoe living in squalor. How could she face her friends?

Five days later, Roscoe was released from the hospital. Zelda had not been back to visit, her head in too much turmoil. However, she did arrange to give him a ride home. She could do that much at least. "Think I can get my car up your dirt road?" she asked.

"Yes. It isn't really so bad, I just told you that so you wouldn't drive up and see my place. The ambulance made it so I'm sure you can." Arriving at his house, Zelda got out, retrieved his crutches from the trunk, then watched him hobble through the yard and up the front steps. At the top, he turned around, and waved a final farewell. "It's been wonderful, he said. No regrets. May you find happiness in your life."

Zelda just stood there. *Wait,* she thought, *haven't I already found happiness? Why should I lose faith now?*

He's everything to me. I'd be crazy to give him up. Suddenly she spun around, waved her arms in the air, swayed her hips back and forth to a throaty tune she was humming and began to dance. Roscoe watched in amazement. Then, a moment later, she ran up the steps, eased around him and through the door. As she entered the house, she took off her jacket, throwing it on top of the other stuff lining the hall. She didn't stop there but moved down the hall, pulling off her top and tossing it aside as well, followed by her bra. Suddenly she was out of her jeans and her panties, throwing them every which way. Arms above her head and still humming, she pranced au naturel down the narrow corridor as Roscoe hung on his crutches, watched and grinned like a man reborn.

Silver Threads

So quiet, the dawn woods. She side-stepped frozen puddles, fearful of shattering a fragile silence. So still and cold. She heard the whisper of crumbling leaves discarded by skeletal limbs, leaves drifting down to expire on the frosty ground. Yesterday had been warm, but now, an October morning had stolen the sun and chilled her bones. Birds no longer chirped. The hum of insects had faded away days ago. As season follows season, winter would soon arrive. A breath of air rustled the icy white grass.

She neither saw nor heard signs of life until surprised, she came upon a shimmering silver thread, almost invisible, stretched across the path. She had walked this trail last evening without so much as a hint of cobwebs brushing her skin. This delicate silk strand must have been constructed in the night, while she lay sleeping all warm in her bed. The mercury had been sliding up and down for several fickle days until, bit by bit, the last remnants of summer had been finally put to sleep. And yet, here was evidence of a determined survivor. How had *he* managed to fend off the deadly cold, carrying out his work against all odds? How did *he* escape his fate?

Tangles of thorny bushes, on either side of the path, supported the ends of his spidery filament. A search through prickly branches, looking for the secretive spinner, turned up nothing. Perhaps the tiny fellow's brief life was over and this but a tribute to his fleeting existence. Had he known the end was near and yet, driven by instinct, kept on doing what he only knew how to do – or had it been a deliberate last attempt to capture a meal and so live another day? Maybe he was still there, hidden under a twig, waiting and hoping to snare one more morsel.

Ducking low, she crawled carefully under his lifeline and continued her walk. Why did this delicate web suddenly become so important, for in past years, she would have broken straight through it? What great change could the tiny spider have worked on this casual passerby?

Autumn thoughts streaked through her mind like sun rays through the clouds. Approaching her winter years, perspective was shifting. As she ambled along over the cold, crunchy ground, she began to wonder. "What other lifelines have I failed to see as I journeyed through the years? Is not each life like that silver thread? Have I honored my neighbor for his life's work as she or he deserved? Have I sought to leave their legacy intact? Preoccupied, I have been blind to others."

Like wind-blown leaves, her thoughts fluttered about, then gently settled. With gathering years, she walked the cold, soon to be wintry forest, aware now of the need to pay heed to other people's stories, to support their dreams – for were their lives and legacies not similar to silver threads and equally worth saving?

The End

I love connecting with my readers and finding out how you feel about my stories. If you enjoyed this book, please leave a review on Amazon.com. for: *The Other Way, A Short Story Collection.*

I would like to suggest, if you liked these stories, to follow this book with: *By The Way, Short Stories by Caperton Tissot,* available on Amazon both in paperback and in kindle.

About the Author

Caperton Tissot's writing life, preceded by years of work in healthcare, ceramics, and environmental advocacy, reflects an abiding interest in small communities and nature. Her work includes publications in journals and newspapers, plus several books of history, fiction, poetry, memoir and short stories, including a children's book. She and her husband live in the Adirondacks, where Tissot balances an outdoor lifestyle with an indoor writing vocation. For contact and more information, visit www.SnowyOwlPress.com.

Bibliography

***By The Way; Short Stories by Caperton Tissot*, 2020**
Fascinating tales to hold the reader enthralled through all
the twists and turns

***Pirates on the Saranac*, 2019**
A children's story of raft adventures on a river

***On Thin Ice; The Life and Times of a North Woods
Caretaker*, 2018**
Mystery, fun and sorrow, this book has it all

***Kicking Leaves; the Contrarian Life of a Yankee Rebel*,
2018**
Short humorous but thoughtful memoir of a rebellious
woman

***The Beat Within; Poetry Another Round*, 2017**
Poetry like music that speaks to the soul

***Adirondack Flashes and Floaters; A River of Verse*, 2014**
Reflecting on the meaning of life in the North Country

**Saranac Lake's Ice Palace; A History of Winter
Carnival's Crown Jewel, 2012**
Photos and text explain the why, how, what and where of
the Palace
(available only at: www.SnowyOwlPress.com)

***Adirondack Ice; A Cultural and Natural History*, 2010**
Photos and stories of the astonishing economic influence
of ice on the North Country

***History between the Lines; Women's Lives and Saranac Lake Customs*, 2007**
How unsung women quietly went about shaping their community's future

Available on Amazon and at www.SnowyOwlPress.com

9 781916 696389